The Snow Baby

by Margaret Hillert

Illustrated by Liz Dauber

DEAR CAREGIVER, The *Beginning-to-Read* series is a carefully written collection of classic readers you may remember from your own childhood. Each book features text comprised of common sight words to provide your child ample practice reading the words that appear most frequently in written text. The many additional details in the pictures enhance the story and offer the opportunity for you to help your child expand oral language and develop comprehension.

Begin by reading the story to your child, followed by letting him or her read familiar words and soon your child will be able to read the story independently. At each step of the way, be sure to praise your reader's efforts to build his or her confidence as an independent reader. Discuss the pictures and encourage your child to make connections between the story and his or her own life. At the end of the story, you will find reading activities and a word list that will help your child practice and strengthen beginning reading skills.

Above all, the most important part of the reading experience is to have fun and enjoy it!

Shannon Cannon

Shannon Cannon,
Literacy Consultant

Norwood House Press • P.O. Box 316598 • Chicago, Illinois 60631
For more information about Norwood House Press please visit our website at *www.norwoodhousepress.com* or call 866-565-2900.

LIBRARY OF CONGRESS CATALOGING-IN-PUBLICATION DATA
　　Hillert, Margaret.
　　　The snow baby / by Margaret Hillert; illustrated by Liz Dauber. — Rev.
　　and expanded library ed.
　　　　p. cm. — (Beginning-to-read book)
　　　Summary: Two children play in the snow and find a furry surprise. Includes
　　reading activities.
　　　ISBN-13: 978-1-59953-045-1 (library binding : alk. paper)
　　　ISBN-10: 1-59953-045-7 (library binding : alk. paper)
　　　[1. Snow—Fiction.] I. Dauber, Liz, ill. II. Title. III. Series: Hillert,
　　Margaret. Beginning to read series. Easy stories.
　　　PZ7.H558Sn 2007
　　　[E]—dc22　　　　　　　　　　　　　2006007891

Come here.
Oh, come here.
See it snow.
Down, down, down it comes.

Snow, snow, snow.
See it snow.
We want to play in it.
It is fun to play in.

Oh, oh.
I can not find something.
Something red is not here.
Where is it?
I can not play.

Oh, I see it.
Here it is.
My red one is here.
I can play in the snow.

Look, look.
Little ones and big ones.
See the snow come down.
Run, run, run.

We can make snowballs.
Big, big snowballs.
Work, work, work.

Oh, oh.
I want one to go up here.
I can not make it go.

Here, here.
It is too big for you.
I can help you.
We two can make it go up.

Here is a little one.
It can go up here.
We can make something funny.
It is big and funny.

13

We can make a snow house, too.
Work, work.
Make a big house.

See me.
See me.
It is fun up here.
Come up, up, up.

One, two, three – jump.
We can jump into the snow.
Find me.
Find me.

Oh, my.
You look funny.
I look funny.
It is fun to play in the snow.

Oh, look.
Here is something.
The big one is me.
The little one is you.

And look here.
I see little spots.
One, two, three.
Three little spots in the snow.

Come, come.
We want to see where
the little spots go.
Look here, look here.

I see something.
It is little.
Is it a little snowball?

Oh, it is a baby.
A little snow baby.
Where is the mother?
Can you find the mother?

The mother is not here.
Come, little baby.
Come to me.
You can come to my house.
Away we go.

Mother, Mother.
Here is a little baby.
It can not run in the snow.
It is too little.

25

It can come into the house.
It can run and play in here.
We want it.
We want the snow baby.

READING REINFORCEMENT

The following activities support the findings of the National Reading Panel that determined the most effective components for reading instruction are: Phonemic Awareness, Phonics, Vocabulary, Fluency, and Text Comprehension.

Phonemic Awareness: The /sn/ sound

Sound Substitution: Say the words on the left to your child. Ask your child to repeat the word, changing the first sound to /sn/:

tap = snap	more = snore	pack = snack	rip = snip
peak = sneak	rug = snug	sail = snail	juggle = snuggle

Phonics: The letter S

1. Demonstrate how to form the letters **S** and **s** for your child.

2. Have your child practice writing **S** and **s** at least three times each.

3. Ask your child to point to the words in the book that start with the letter **s**.

4. Write down the following words and ask your child to circle the letter **s** in each word:

see	snow	send	yes	salt
sort	kiss	soft	past	bus
less	list	mustard	so	this

Vocabulary: Snowy Day

1. Ask your child to draw a picture of him or herself playing outside on a snowy day.

2. Ask your child to point to the objects in the picture and name them.

3. Label the pictures with the words provided by your child.

4. Ask your child to tell a story to go with the picture using the word labels.

5. If your child has trouble drawing the picture, help him or her to come up with a list of words first and then draw a picture to go with them.

Fluency: Echo Reading

1. Reread the story to your child at least two more times while your child tracks the print by running a finger under the words as they are read. Ask your child to read the words he or she knows with you.

2. Reread the story, stopping after each sentence or page to allow your child to read (echo) what you have read. Repeat echo reading and let your child take the lead.

Text Comprehension: Discussion Time

1. Ask your child to retell the sequence of events in the story.

2. To check comprehension, ask your child the following questions:
   - How did the boy and girl get ready to go out in the snow?
   - How did the boy and girl make a house?
   - What were the spots in the snow?
   - What do you think the snow baby is?
   - Why did the boy and girl want to bring the snow baby home?
   - Can you think of other things you can do in the snow?

WORD LIST

The Snow Baby uses the 50 words listed below.

This list can be used to practice reading the words that appear in the text. You may wish to write the words on index cards and use them to help your child build automatic word recognition. Regular practice with these words will enhance your child's fluency in reading connected text.

a	help	not	the
and	here		three
away	house	oh	to
		one (s)	too
baby	I		two
big	in	play	
	into		up
can	is	red	
come (s)	it	run	want
			we
down	jump	see	where
		snow	work
find	little	snowball (s)	
for	look	something	you
fun		spots	
funny	make		
	me		
go	mother		
	my		

ABOUT THE AUTHOR Margaret Hillert has written over 80 books for children who are just learning to read. Her books have been translated into many different languages and over a million children throughout the world have read her books. She first started writing poetry as a child and has continued to write for children and adults throughout her life. A first grade teacher for 34 years, Margaret is now retired from teaching and lives in Michigan where she likes to write, take walks in the morning, and care for her three cats.

Photograph by Glenna Washburn

ABOUT THE ADVISER Shannon Cannon contributed the activities pages that appear in this book. Shannon serves as a literacy consultant and provides staff development to help improve reading instruction. She is a frequent presenter at educational conferences and workshops. Prior to this she worked as an elementary school teacher and as president of a curriculum publishing company.